The Ten Lives of Hector, The Cat!

The Ten Lives of Hector, The Cat!

JANE L. KING

ISBN: 9798698171669 (paperback)

Illustrated by Kayla Phan

Have you ever met anyone who is completely nondescript? You have now! I want to introduce you to Sheila. Sheila lives a completely boring life in a small village, twenty miles east of the outskirts of London. She has lived in this village, called Upper Rayford, for all of the fifty-six years of her life.

There is nothing I can tell you about Sheila that would interest you. She is pale, with fluffy, medium-length gray hair. She has a few freckles on her face. She is of medium height and wears longish gray skirts, with gray cardigans over crumpled grayish-white cotton blouses. She also wears gray socks, with worn, blackish-gray shoes. Sheila has no family or friends. She is on a fixed income and has few pleasures. That's Sheila!

Sheila has something very special in her life, though, and that is Hector, The Cat! Hector is the opposite of Sheila. He is the most beautiful ginger (orange) tabby cat you could ever hope to see. He is growing into approximately twenty pounds in weight, and it is all muscle. He has a broad face and amazingly long whiskers. Of course, Hector has the classic "M" sign on his forehead.

Everything about Hector is perfect. Many times when Sheila and Hector are in the garden together, and people walk by, they see only Hector, and speak only to Hector. Sheila does not mind, though, because she sees and speaks only to Hector as well.

As I mentioned, Hector has a different life to Sheila. So far, he has lived ten lives, and he is still counting. He has lived the life of an Aztec, a Buddhist monk, a Japanese samurai, and an Indian raja. He has traveled to some of the most interesting countries of the world. This story is about one of the ten lives of Hector, The Cat!

Hector's life began inauspiciously. He can remember only vaguely now the warmth of his mother. Something terrible had happened to her, and he could not bear to think about it. He agreed for Sheila to take him into her home because she had lovely warm hands and stroked him in such a beautifully kind way. Although Sheila appeared relatively nondescript, she had a warm and generous heart, and she loved cats more than her own life.

Before I begin to tell you about Hector's first life, he would want me to mention his closest cat friends. He found them while exploring the neighborhood one day, after he had grown into a confident and friendly young cat. There were three of them, and he spent a good deal of time making friends with them because as all cats know—and some humans know—cats tend to be particularly selective about who they choose as their friends and family.

The names of Hector's closest cat friends are Doogy, Sammi, and Charlie. Hector remembers quite clearly when he first met Doogy many years ago. Doogy was a true beauty! She had long, luxurious fur and perfect black-and-white markings. It was love at first sight for Hector!

Doogy, though, was somewhat timid at first and ran away from the window every time he went toward her. Over time, he broke down her reserve, and she began to trust him.

As for Sammi, she was three times the size of petite Doogy. She was completely black, with dense fur and the brightest green eyes Hector had ever seen. She was more of a queen of cats than a princess like Doogy. From time to time, Hector would meet with his girlfriends, and he would tell them stories about his exploits. It was difficult to tell these two friends stories, though, because Doogy was impressed by daring and adventure, but Sammi was impressed by achievements.

Similar to Queen Elizabeth I, Sammi wanted Hector not only to explore and have adventures, but also to return and bring riches for her to enjoy. She especially liked the spicy tuna dishes he had returned from India with. (Of course, it was Hector's secret that this food actually came from the Indian restaurant in their village, which was called The Magical Sambar. In this restaurant, he had made friends with one of the waiters, who would regularly save spicy dishes for him. Hector loved Indian food!)

Hector's third friend was Charlie. They had met almost by accident as Charlie was making his rounds through the village alleyways one day. The beautiful thing about Charlie was that he did not have an aggressive bone in his body. He was built like a giant—much larger than Hector—with lots of white and sandy-colored fluffy fur. He was a peaceful soul, though, and liked nothing better than spending the day with friends in the sun. Hector had taken Charlie on a few voyages, but Charlie only wanted to make friends with others and lie in the sun with them. Hector sometimes found this quite aggravating, but, because Hector had such a generous nature, he accepted Charlie as he was and loved him for it.

So, this was Hector's group: Doogy, Sammi, and Charlie. Hector knew many other cats, as he did dogs and other animals, and even humans, and some of these were very important to him. His nature was such that he enjoyed meeting and learning from others. This special group of friends, though, made up his family, together with Sheila—although there was one major difference between his friends and Sheila. Hector could

trust his friends with the knowledge of his adventures, but he did not feel he could trust Sheila. She was not a particularly imaginative human being, and she preferred him to be a more traditional type of cat. He would not want to upset her in any way by revealing something so different as the fact he was a time-traveling cat!

When Hector began to travel, he always shared his experiences with Sammi and Doogy on his return. It was quite miraculous really that Hector had found a magical way to travel from the home he shared with Sheila. Sheila had a very large dictionary that she left open on her desk. This desk sometimes (as much as is possible in England, given that it rains often)

was flooded with sun rays and warmth, which came through the window above the desk.

Like most cats, Hector loved sunshine, and he loved the warmth it produced. He would lie on the large open book and drift away into a pleasurable world of dreams. This is how he began his journeys: in a deep sleep induced by the sunshine and the warmth.

As Hector dreamed in the sunshine, something truly amazing would happen— as he often tells me. There would be a word on one of the two pages which would transform his life into something quite beyond belief. I want to give you an example, and this was the first time that Hector time-traveled. One day when Hector was asleep on the dictionary, it was open to the

"E" section. One of the words in this section was "Egypt."

As an aside, it just so happens that Hector already had a great interest in Egypt. He is not an intellectual, and he is certainly not an academic like his distant cousin Professor Topsy Turvey. He had learned a lot from Professor Turvey, though, because she is from Egypt. She belongs to the ancient Mau tribe of cats that guarded the pyramids. Hector knew, then, about the cats in ancient Egypt and the pyramids, and the pharaohs. But he didn't know much more than this.

Another interesting fact is that Hector can trace his roots to ancient Greece. Catistorians have long believed that Hector of Troy was part cat. This was due to the influence of the ancient

Egyptian Cat Goddess—Bastet.   Cat scholars have worked for many years to prove this connection. Everyone knows that Hector was a courageous and virtuous Trojan.   His parents reputedly were King Priam and Queen Hecuba. Catistorians, though, believed that his mother was actually Bastet.

The First Life of Hector, The Cat!

Returning to our story, then, Hector's first experience with time-traveling was to ancient Egypt. As you will remember, this began when Hector fell asleep on the dictionary in Sheila's study, and as often happens to humans as well when they see an entry in a dictionary, the word "Egypt" entered his mind. For humans, this might lead to discovering more information about Egypt, but for our Hector, he was actually transported to Egypt.

When I asked him if he knew he was traveling to Egypt, he told me that he did not really know about the journey or experience it. Cats have a special sense that allows them to travel through space and human time, and they travel completely unseen. When they travel in this way, they simply dream the journey, and many time-traveling cats can be seen moving their paws and flicking their tails—and meowing slightly—as they travel. Often their journeys are interrupted because humans wake them up. Fortunately, Sheila was much too respectful of Hector to wake him up. She loved to look in the room and see him

asleep on the book in the sun. It made her
heart feel as warm as toast.

Imagine Hector, then, swooshing through time and space, making his way to Egypt. This was not intentional in any way. Because Hector left himself open to traveling anywhere, the page of the dictionary and the entries on it determined his destination. Imagine if we all did this, and were completely spontaneous about our journeys? If you were to be free in this way, where would you go at this very moment?

When Hector finally arrived in Egypt, he woke up suddenly in a very warm climate on a carpet of soft sand. As he came to, he almost immediately became aware of a massive stone structure looming some distance in front of him. When he saw this structure, he stood up and slowly looked at the building, beginning at the bottom and following it all the way to the top. He had never seen such an enormous structure. And it was very wide at the bottom, tapering to a point at the top.

At first, Hector thought he had found his way to the mythical land of the giants. He was relieved then to see some humans walking about who were of a normal size. He noticed, though, that these humans were wearing different types of clothes than he was used to seeing. Most of the men wore short white skirts tied at the waist, and the women wore dresses made of the same material. Both women and men wore sandals. Some of the people looked important and had thick black hair—although this hair looked more like a wig. Some people were carrying goods on top of their heads, and he saw oxen pulling carts. From looking at these people and their activities, there was no doubt in Hector's mind that he had traveled back in time to another century. He had no idea at this point, though, how far in time he had traveled.

As he looked again at the massive stone structure, he suddenly remembered seeing the picture of a pyramid that his cousin Professor Turvey had shown him in England. As he walked around the area, he could see other pyramids in the distance and something stunning that looked as though it was a giant lion. The face of this massive statue, though, was human. He was seeing the amazing Sphinx! All cats knew about the Sphinx and could recognize it because its body represented a lion—king of all cats. (Catistorians in the present age as well have used this statue to help prove the connection between Hector of Troy and the Egyptian cat goddess, Bastet.)

It felt to Hector like a sacred place. He remembered Professor Turvey telling him about the pyramids, saying that they were, in essence, the largest type of graves in the world. Although pyramids were built in other parts of the world too, the ones familiar to most of us are those in Egypt. Hector had time-traveled, then, to Egypt. Hector could not have been happier. He was so interested in everything, and to have come to this country, with its incredible history and civilization, thrilled him. Hector was curious to learn and to know everything about this new world. As we all know, curiosity is something all cats have. It leads them to have wonderful adventures, but it can also be risky because they have no fear about the final possible result if one wrong turn is taken.

While Hector was looking around, shading his eyes because the sun was so bright, he did not notice that he had been seen and that he had been quickly and quietly surrounded by Egyptian cats carrying bows and arrows. There were probably ten of them staring at him. And they all looked similar—and that is, a lot like Professor Turvey. As mentioned, she came from Egypt and is an Egyptian Mau. They looked like extremely smart tabby cats, but with the most erect cat body type Hector had ever seen. He could see clearly that although their backs were striped, the other side of their bodies was a golden desert color with beautiful black spots—similar to his cousin's coloring, but even more dramatic. Their heads were more upright, and

narrower, than his own. They looked positively regal!

It was interesting that these cats had such an important role in Egypt. They were obviously guards in this impressive region of pyramids and monuments. Hector knew, though, that these cats had not been given this role. They had taken it. Cats are well known to be independent and capable of living in the wild. When they live with humans, it is a choice. This has always been true throughout their long history on Earth. They are not like dogs and other animals who have been domesticated by humans.

Here was our Hector, then, surrounded by Mau cat warriors, who were looking at him directly with their bright yellow-green eyes—with interest, but also with daring and courage. They were ready to take whatever action was necessary to protect themselves and the sacred area they guarded. The leader of this group of cats spoke first to Hector, saying, "Who are you, and where have you come from? I am the leader of the cats here in this sacred place."

(Hector was thinking how stately this leader of cats looked, with her perfect posture and her large, piercing blue eyes. There was a sense about her that she was extremely intelligent. She was taller than the cats she commanded. Her language was precise, and she was obviously well educated.)

Hector spoke slowly. "My name is Hector, and I am from England. I am pleased to be here and to meet you."

The leader asked, "Where is England? We have never heard of that place."

Hector said, "I want to ask you

something first, if you don't mind. Where am I, and what year is it?"

"You are in Giza in Egypt, and the year is 1469."

Hector took a moment to think about this, knowing that he was in an ancient place because life was so very different. He looked about him again, glancing at the Sphinx and at the pyramids close by and in the distance. He recognized them from photographs, but they looked different—the pyramids looked almost new, and the Sphinx was intact. Its face was perfect. He quickly deduced then that this was 1469 B.C.E., or approximately 3,500 years in the past.

Hector was not shocked by this realiza- tion. For a cat who time-travels, there is no sense of surprise, and our Hector was fearless as well. He could not wait to find out more and to make friends with these ancient Egyptian cats.

These cats, of course, knew about time-traveling cats. They had never seen such a beautiful cat as Hector, though—with his perfectly marked, bright orange and sandy-colored striped fur. In fact, Hector could see that some of the cats were looking at him amorously.

"So," he said to the leader, "may I ask your name?"

"My name is Purrosophos. I am the leader of the cats who guard the pyramids, the connected buildings, and the statues in Giza. We have been appointed to do this work by Queen Hatshepsut, who is pharaoh of all Egypt and beyond."

Hector bowed. Purrosophos then asked him again, "Where is England?"

Hector replied, "It is a country a great distance from Egypt. On behalf of our leader, I would like to invite you to visit me there in the future."

Purrosophos said, "That is very gracious of you. Thank you."

Many of you will know that in ancient Egypt, cats were revered. They were viewed as having special powers and were allowed—even encouraged—to participate in the lives of Egyptians as they pleased. Similar to cows in India, they were treated as special because they had a close connection with the gods and goddesses. In fact, in ancient Egypt, cats represented the gods and goddesses (including the goddess Bastet, of course).

I want you to imagine with me how humans felt about cats in ancient Egypt. They believed they were divine in nature and should be cherished for their special place in this world—somewhere between the Earth and eternity. When you look at cats today, can you imagine a time when they were uniformly treated by humans with such respect and kindness? Perhaps we can learn an important lesson from those ancient times.

Returning to our story now, and to Hector, I am sure you can imagine the reaction of Egyptians to this orange (ginger) cat from England. Purrosophos was quick to introduce Hector to other cat leaders, as well as to some humans who had connections in the court of the pharaoh. It was not long, therefore, before Hector was invited to meet Queen Hatshepsut.

When he arrived at the palace, which was the grandest place he had ever seen, with gold and marble everywhere, he was amazed by it. As he walked into the grand hall, where the Queen met her subjects, Hector could see her in the distance, sitting at the end of the room on a massive throne made of gold. She wore a tall white crown, and her eyes looked very large, because of the black line painted around each of them and her thick black eyebrows. Black lines extended from her eyes and eyebrows toward her ears. The effect was mesmerizing.

As Hector moved toward the Queen, he could see that she had noticed him. Everyone made space for him to walk forward. She was looking at him as though he was something very special, and she beckoned him onward.

Then the Queen spoke to him: "I have heard of you. You are Hector, The Cat! I have never seen a cat who is so completely the color of gold. Come closer to me and let me stroke your fur."

Hector moved toward her, kissed the ground, and climbed the steps to her feet.

He was then lifted by her attendants so that she could look directly into his eyes. He could tell that this Queen was special. She had an openness about her, and a warmth, although she was obviously bold at the same time. The Queen gently stroked Hector's fur. She pronounced that he was her special cat and she would make him a lord of Egypt. From now on he would be called Hectortutem I. She also told him that she had a mission for him, which he must accept, in order to prove his courage and his loyalty to her.

It may be important to know that Queen Hatshepsut had proclaimed herself pharaoh of Egypt. It was unusual for a woman to have this role. She was leading Egypt for an interim period because her stepson, Tuthmosis III, was too young to be king. She appointed herself pharaoh by claiming the gods required it. As pharaoh, she was different from the men who had ruled before her, focusing on exploration of other lands and creating a time of peace and prosperity—without war—in Egypt.

When Hector heard this, it reminded him of England's Queen Elizabeth I.

Of course, similar to Queen Elizabeth I, Queen Hatshepsut had enemies who wanted to overthrow her and take the crown for themselves.

Hector was quite keen to learn about the Queen's mission for him. He loved adventures, as you know. He told the Queen that he would undertake any mission she had in mind for him. The Queen told him that she wanted him to lead a special delegation to Nubia. She had decided to reach out because she wanted to make a trade deal with them. For this purpose, she would appoint him Ambassador to Nubia.

(At this point, Hector began thinking to himself about Nubia. He had learned about the Nubians, who were the most beautifully colored humans, with an advanced civilization that had existed at the same time as the Egyptian civilization.

History tended to overlook the Nubians and their contribution, though. He was pleased, then, to have the opportunity to learn all about this ancient civilization and about the cats and humans who had helped to build it.)

The Queen next instructed one of her cat lieutenants to prepare a ceremony for the appointment of Hectortutem I as the Ambassador to Nubia. She also instructed a scribe to prepare a document to represent her appointment of Hector. This document, full of hieroglyphs—or pictures of the Queen, and the palace, and Hector—would be given to the Nubians by Hector on behalf of the Queen.

The ceremony was a grand affair at which flutes, lutes, drums, and other instruments were played, while a fine linen carpet was rolled out along the path to the Queen's throne. Hector was adorned in a full-length linen tunic. His tail was carefully allowed to protrude through a hole cut in the back of the tunic. He was given a spear made of gold and an Egyptian headdress made of gold. Now he was ready to walk along the carpet toward the Queen to accept this great honor of becoming Ambassador to Nubia.

As Hector walked toward the Queen, the cats and the humans to the right and the left of the carpet bowed down to him. They stayed in this position until the Queen had taken his two top paws in her hands and solemnly pronounced him Ambassador to Nubia. She then placed a necklace with a wadjet eye around his neck to keep him safe.

Following the ceremony, delicious food was served for every cat and human in attendance, together with large cups of wine. After dinner, they enjoyed performers who played music and danced for their pleasure.

At the end of the evening, Hector was shown to his beautiful room in the palace. This had been specially built for important cat guests. It contained the softest bed imaginable, together with a private area for personal hygiene. There were thick carpets for scratching purposes and running water for drinking. The food was the most delicious he had ever tasted. Hector was sure that it had been imported from Cat Heaven.

Now, will you join with me in imagining Hector in this beautiful room? Have you ever noticed how cats make everything around them even more beautiful? What magical qualities do you believe they have that make this possible?

On the morning after his appointment, following a good night's sleep, Hector faced the challenging task of planning his trip to Nubia and choosing who would accompany him. He needed some Egyptian cats who were familiar with the Nubians and could communicate with Nubian cats to pave the way for him. As a first step, then, he sent a messenger to ask Purrosophos to come to the palace to meet with him. When she arrived, these two cats from different worlds greeted each other warmly. Purrosophos first told Hector that he must call her Purro. This was the short name used by her family and closest friends.

"Purro," Hector said, "I'm sure you've heard that I have been appointed to go to Nubia on behalf of the Queen."

"Yes, I know," she said. "It is a great honor."

"Can you help me prepare the way so that my visit can be successful?"

"I will be pleased to help you in any way I can. I do know of three cats who would be excellent for you to work with. They are originally from Nubia, and I am sure they would be pleased to share their knowledge and advice with you."

"Thank you, Purro. Would you send them to meet with me here in the palace?"

"Yes, of course, my dear Hector. I will take my leave for now."

The two cats, who had become close friends, parted company.

Over the course of the next two weeks, Hector met with and worked with the three Nubian cats, who were invaluable to him as he gradually formed the plan for his visit. Finally, the day for his journey arrived, and everyone assembled at the palace loading point along the Nile River. For this journey, the explorers would travel in a boat up the river (which was southward into the continent of Africa).

On the trip southward, the winds would carry them similar to a sailboat in the modern world. For the trip back, they would row northward. The boat was fully loaded with everything needed for this important trip, including very special presents from the Queen to the Nubians. All of the cats and

the human guards had bows and arrows for defense.

After every cat and human had boarded the boat and Hector had taken his place at the front of the boat, the captain of the boat steered it up the River Nile. The land all along the riverbanks was lush and green, and there was a great deal of activity. Hector was interested to see everything! He was excited beyond belief! (Imagine if you or I could have this experience? How wonderful would it be?!)

For two days, the boat moved along toward Nubia without any delays or difficulties. It was on the third day, though, that the boat was attacked from the shoreline by ferocious dogs. A stream of arrows was sent over from both sides of the river by humans, and the dogs were in small boats, rowing very quickly towards Hector's boat.

Hector had to think fast to save his boat, his crew, his mission, and himself. He could only think of calling one of his dog friends from England. Although dogs do not time-travel naturally, Hector had discovered a way to bring his dog friends from England, from time to time, when it was necessary. He took a moment then to communicate through time and space with his friend Alfie. Alfie was a black spaniel, but unlike many spaniels, he was large and very muscular. Hector could see that Alfie was sleeping and was, fortunately, alone. His human mother was out working, obviously.

Alfie loved adventure, but he always had to return to be sure that he was back by the time his mother arrived home. He loved his mother very much and always wanted to show her how much he loved her. Whenever she came home, then, he would show his love by jumping and running about, and he would pick up and carry one of her slippers.

Alfie and his mother had a truly magical bond, but this meant that Alfie could time-travel for only limited periods. Because Hector had to use his own powers to bring dogs from England, time would pass for them in the new location the same as it would at home. This was not true for cats. Hector could be in Egypt for a long time, but Sheila would still see him sleeping on the book for just an afternoon.

Thankfully, Alfie was available and appeared instantaneously at Hector's side. When Alfie arrived, he quickly assessed the situation and took charge of it. He began to howl and grew to become the largest dog you have ever seen. Alfie's howling, by the way, was, when he projected his voice, as loud as a fog horn, but at a much higher pitch. When the ferocious dogs saw this giant warrior dog on the boat, they retreated quickly, as did the humans who had been giving them orders, because they were all terrified. Humans and dogs then quickly disappeared, and Hector could continue the journey. Later, Hector would learn that one of the Queen's rivals had been responsible for this attack. This rival did not want the Queen to be successful as Pharaoh, which would make it easier to overthrow her.

As for Alfie, who had saved the day, he needed to quickly return home to his mother. She was due back at any moment.

He would need to be howling when she drove around the corner to their house so that she knew how much he had missed her. He embraced his friend Hector, and, then, quickly time-traveled back to England.

Thanks to Alfie, the boat was now able to make good time as it headed toward Nubia. On the sixth day of their journey, Hector and his crew were met by a group of Nubian cats sent out by the Nubian leaders to assess whether or not these visitors could be trusted. Egypt had not been a good neighbor and was not trusted by the Nubian leaders. They needed to be sure that the new Pharaoh was trustworthy.

The Nubian cats were sufficiently

impressed by Hector to allow him to fol-
low them to the Nubian leaders. When
Hector saw the leaders, he was amazed by
the beautiful dark color of their skin. They
also wore brightly colored clothes and unusual jewelry. Hector was not usually impressed by humans, but he could see that
these humans were very special.

The leaders asked him to join them in
a circle to discuss his mission and his pro-
posals. As Hector sat with these humans,
he was impressed with the way in which
they conducted themselves and interacted
with him. They were kind and respectful,
and in everything they said, it was clear that
they had deeply held beliefs about the im-
portance of all life, and that they reverently
worshipped their ancestors, gods, and goddesses. Given that the Nubian leaders were

open to forming allegiances with other nations, and to promoting peace throughout their world, the meeting with Hector went extremely well. The Nubian leaders were impressed by Hector and by the gifts he had brought from the Egyptian Queen. They agreed to send a trade delegation back with him to see the Queen.

When Hector returned to the palace with the Nubian delegation, the Queen was very grateful. She honored him greatly—not only for his success on the trade mission but also for thwarting her rival's plot. She told Hector that she loved him so much she wanted him to be mummified when she left this Earth so that he would be with her forever.

As I am sure you know, this was the way cats and humans were preserved for eternity by the Egyptians. After being mummified, Hector would be entombed in the Valley of the Kings, where the Queen was to be buried. After that, the Queen and Hector would travel through the underworld, passing tests as they went along and eventually rising the next morning with the sun for eternity.

Because Hector was now considered to be sacred by the Egyptians, it was important for him to be protected from harm until the day of his departure from life with the Queen. This meant that he could only stay in his room in the palace. His days of adventure were over, and he would never be able to return home to England. He was enclosed in his room in the palace, and everything was done to make him happy. Because of the thickness of the walls, he found he was unable to time-travel out of the palace. At first, Hector felt overcome by sadness. He was upset to leave the Queen, and also, upset not to ever see Sheila and his family and friends again in England.

Hector, though, has the type of personality that will always allow him to rise up to a positive place in order to solve problems and to be happy. As a first step to solve this problem, Hector tried to contact his cousin Professor Turvey, who is one of the most intelligent and knowledgeable cats he knows. Hector knew that she had special powers, and might just be able to help him to escape from Egypt.

He sat comfortably in his room in the morning, then, and concentrated very hard—searching for Professor Turvey in cat space. After a short time, he connected with her mind and communicated his difficulty. Professor Turvey told him to stay quiet, and she would use some of her ancient powers to try to bring him home. As you will remember, Professor Turvey is an Egyptian Mau—directly descended from the ancient Egyptian cats. She carried their special powers within her, but she did not need to use them very much in the modern world.

⁓❦⁓

"Hector, Hector ..." He could hear these words through his consciousness. He was being called. Was it the Queen? No, it was Sheila! (Sheila had broken her rule of never disturbing Hector while he slept because he seemed to be having a nightmare.) Then, he felt her kissing his head and gently stroking his back. He slowly opened his eyes, and there she was! He was home.

Can you imagine how happy and relieved Hector felt to be home again? Have you ever been away for a long time from home? How does it feel when you return? This was how Hector felt at this moment. He was especially relieved as well because he had felt that his life was over in ancient Egypt.

Hector gradually woke up and stretched out on the dictionary, while Sheila stroked him, and talked to him. He rubbed her face and purred a truly royal purr. He was completely content—having had such an amazing adventure, and now being back in his warm and comfortable home with Sheila. He jumped down from the desk, and followed her into the kitchen for his dinner which would taste of home, sweet, home. There was enough time to rest and to remember his adventures before he headed out tomorrow with his gifts for Sammi and his stories for Doogy.

After dinner, Hector sat in front of the fire, and enjoyed the comforts of his home. He did not spend too much time thinking about his close calls in Egypt, and how his curiosity had almost resulted in his mummification. One of his nine lives had been used, but now, he was safely home again.

Printed in Great Britain
by Amazon